DIARY OF A MINECRAFT ZOMBIE

BOOK 32

HAVE YOURSELF A MOULDY MINECRAFT CHRISTMAS

Koala Books
An imprint of Scholastic Australia Pty Limited
PO Box 579 Gosford NSW 2250
ABN 11 000 614 577
www.scholastic.com.au

Part of the Scholastic Group
Sydney • Auckland • New York • Toronto • London • Mexico City
New Delhi • Hong Kong • Buenos Aires • Puerto Rico

Published by Scholastic Australia in 2021.
Text copyright © Zack Zombie Publishing 2021.

A catalogue record for this
book is available from the
NATIONAL LIBRARY OF AUSTRALIA
National Library of Australia

ISBN 978-1-76097-870-9

Typeset in Agent 'C', Potato Cut TT and Maqui.

Printed by McPherson's Printing Group, Maryborough, VIC.

Scholastic Australia's policy, in association with McPherson's Printing Group, is to use
papers that are renewable and made efficiently with wood from responsibly managed
sources, so as to minimise its environmental footprint.

MIX
Paper from
responsible sources
FSC® C001695

The paper in this book is FSC® certified.
FSC® promotes environmentally responsible,
socially beneficial and economically viable
management of the world's forests.

21 22 23 24 25 / 2

DIARY OF A MINECRAFT ZOMBIE

BOOK 32

HAVE YOURSELF A MOULDY MINECRAFT CHRISTMAS

BY
Zack Zombie

Koala Books

THREE NIGHTS BEFORE CHRISTMAS

'It is really hot, man,' Skelee said. 'I don't even have skin and I'm hot.'

'I know!' I said. 'What's up with this weather? It doesn't usually change in this biome.'

'Yeah...' Skelee just shook his head. 'Must be a **GLITCH.**'

We both stared up at the night sky. It looked the same as it does every night. So why was it so hot?

Skelee and I were walking home from school. But I wasn't ready to go home yet, so I decided to take a detour and visit Steve.

'I'm gonna head this way.'

'Off to hang out with Steve?' Skelee asked.

I just nodded and waved. 'See ya tomorrow, Skelee!'

It took a few minutes of **TRUDGING** through the Forest before I heard the familiar THWACK! THWACK! THWACK! of Steve chopping down trees.

It's so weird that Steve never gets sick of chopping down trees. But then I never get tired of scaring Villagers, so what do I know?

Tree punching pro

'Hey, Steve,' I said.

THWACK!

'Hey, Zombie!' THWACK! 'What's poppin'?'

I started counting the joints that had been popping out lately. 'Both shoulders, one knee and my back.' Steve laughed at me.

See? Weird.

'Anything new going on?' he asked.

'Just school, you know.' I dropped my backpack onto the ground and slumped down next to it. 'It's weirdly hot, hey?'

'Yeah!' Steve said excitedly. 'I love this weather. It reminds me of CHRISTMAS.'

I stared at Steve. 'Huh?'

'I even modified my Furnace into a barbeque. See?' Steve grabbed my arm and pulled me over to something that looked like it used to be a Furnace but the top had been ripped off and there were metal racks added over the flames. There was a **RAW CHICKEN** roasting on it.

'I don't understand. What does hot weather and barbeque have to do with each other? And what's Christmas?' I asked.

'What's Christmas?!' Steve exclaimed. 'Oh man, it's the best! You get presents and eat food and spend the whole time doing nothing.'

'Oh, so like a birthday?' I asked.

'Kind of!' Steve said. 'But like, it's extra special, because Santa Claus delivers presents to everyone. And it always happens at the hottest time of the year.'

'What's a **SANTA CLAUS?**'

Steve dropped his Axe in shock. 'Who! Santa Claus is a "Who", not a "What"! He's an **OLD, FAT GUY** in a red suit and funny hat, who flies on a magic sleigh pulled by flying reindeer, and says "Ho Ho Ho" and leaves presents. And as a thank you, we leave cookies out for him. And maybe a Carrot for his reindeer.'

I gave Steve a puzzled look. 'Now you're pulling my leg. What's a rain deer? Deer that only come out in the rain?'

Steve checked on the roast chicken. While he spoke, he poked at it until he decided it was cooked. He offered me some, but I used to be a Chicken Jockey... so no thanks.

That's all yours, Steve!

'So, Santa Claus has a whole set-up,' Steve said as he munched on his barbequed chicken. 'Reindeer, elves, a factory to make the presents and a flying sleigh to deliver them to everyone around the WORLD, so they are ready for everyone to wake up to on Christmas Day. It's a **HUMAN STORY** from out there,' Steve waved his hand vaguely at the sky. 'But it's fun to celebrate in Minecraft too.'

'I still don't get it. Santa gives everyone presents for free? What's in it for him?' I asked.

'Well, not everyone. He only gives them presents if they've been **GOOD ALL YEAR.**'

I gulped. 'What about, for example, a Zombie mob kid who hasn't been good?' I quickly thought back to all the times I had been grounded this year. Would Santa know about that?

'Well, Santa has a Naughty and Nice List. If you're on the Naughty List, you won't know until Christmas Day when you wake up with a **LUMP OF COAL** under your tree instead of presents.'

'Wait, what?' I was even more confused now. 'Which tree? I gotta get a tree?'

'Of course! Where do you think Santa puts the presents? Here, why don't you take this one?' Steve pointed at the tree he had been chopping down.

'What do I do with it?' I asked.

'Put some **LIGHTS** on it. Then Santa will know where to put the presents. And then on Christmas Day there will be presents under it!'

'And Santa Claus will put them there?'

'Yup,' Steve nodded. But then he paused mid-nod. 'But maybe it won't be Santa Claus exactly. I heard a rumour that there's a different Santa for mobs. He's not a Human and he doesn't have reindeer!'

'Wait, really?' I leaned forward.

'Yup. One Villager told me that he was a Creeper! And he calls himself **SANTA CREEPS.**' He finished off the last bite of his barbequed chicken. 'Why don't you come over on Christmas and we can have a barbeque together and you can tell me all about it?'

'Sure!' I said. At least that sounded real and not made up. Honestly, it all sounded made up, but I don't think Steve would trick me like that. 'So I need to take this tree home with me and then put lights in it?'

Steve nodded. He helped me drag the tree to the edge of the Forest, but then he had to go. So I dragged the tree the rest of the way home by myself. This had **BETTER BE WORTH IT!**

When I finally got there, I propped the tree up in the front garden.

'Okay,' I said to myself. 'Now I gotta put some lights in it.'

I headed into the garage and dug around until I found some old lightbulbs in a box. I took the box out the front and started randomly shoving the lightbulbs into the tree.

'There!' I stepped back and looked at my handiwork. There were lightbulbs balanced amongst the tree's branches, and the tree was leaning to one side.

My **EYE SOCKETS** widened in delight. I could feel myself becoming... happier? Was this what it felt like to be excited for Christmas?

I wanted everyone to feel this good, so I decided to tell everyone about Christmas! But I would need some help...

TWO NIGHTS BEFORE CHRISTMAS

As soon as I got to Scare School, I told the guys everything I had learned about Christmas.

'Wait, so the hot weather's not a glitch?' Skelee asked.

'Nope!' I shook my head. 'At the **HOTTEST** time of the year, an old mob named Santa Creeps will give us presents! And we're supposed to spend the whole night eating barbequed food.' Then, I told them about the tree I'd dragged home and decorated.

'Wow,' Slimey said.

'Why does he give us presents?'
Slimey asked.

'I dunno!' I said. 'Apparently he's just a **REALLY NICE MOB.**'

'How do I get a present from
Santa Creeps?' Creepy asked.

'You just gotta be good! And you
gotta have a tree.'

'A tree?' Skelee asked.

'Yeah. You gotta find and

DECORATE a tree so Santa has something to put the presents under.'

'I want a tree!' Slimey said. 'How do I get one?'

'I can show you!' I said.

It took a while, but we found trees for Slimey, Skelee and Creepy. While we were getting their trees set up, Principal Hogskins walked by and asked what we were doing. She seemed very interested and asked how to get Santa to give her a present too.

Even the Principal wants some of this free gift action!

Then Creepy said he had to tell his cousin, Ellie, about Santa to make sure she had a tree too.

Slimey and Skelee also wanted to tell mobs they knew, so everyone had a tree in time to get a present from Santa.

They were yelling, **'CHRISTMAS IS COMING,** get a tree!' as they left. So I guess all of

Minecraft would know about Christmas and Santa Creeps soon enough.

It looked like my friends had the telling part covered, so I went to hang out with Steve and learn more about Christmas.

Steve was chopping Wood when I went over after school. Surprise, surprise! And he had a pile of Wood neatly **STACKED** next to him.

'Steve!' I called out.

'Zombie!' he yelled in reply.

'I'm here to learn more about Christmas.'

'What else do you want to know?' Steve asked, putting down his Axe.

'Slimey, Creepy, Skelee were asking me about Santa, and, well, what are the **RULES?**'

'What do you mean "rules"?'

'You know, the rules of Christmas. To make sure we win.'

Steve chuckled and shook his head. 'There are no rules! Do whatever you want. The only things that matter for Christmas are: you gotta have presents, it's gotta be hot, you gotta eat yummy food and you gotta be happy. And you have to do this with the ones you love.'

'Love?' I asked. **'YUCK,** I don't love anyone.'

'What about your family? Your mum and dad and Wesley?' Steve asked.

'Oh yeah, well, of course. Obviously I love them.' I said, shrugging my arms.

'Then you have everything you need

to make Christmas GREAT!'

'But how do you **WIN?** I asked.

'Win? You don't win! There's
nothing to win at Christmas, it
isn't a competition.'

'What's the point of it, then?'

'It's all about Christmas spirit!'
Steve explained. 'Doing fun things
and feeling good.'

'And presents?' I checked. I
wanted to make sure I had the
presents bit right. 'I get presents?'

'Yeah! Everyone gets presents.'

I dunno. Something about Christmas sounded **TOO GOOD TO BE TRUE.**

I hung out with Steve for a bit longer before I left to go home.

I was trudging through the Forest, thinking about Christmas, when I heard a jingle. It sounded like bells, clinking together. But I was in the Forest. Who would have bells? And why would they clink them together?

I froze.

Maybe it was **PLAYERS...** The mean kind, not like Steve.

I twisted my face into a scary expression. It had been a little while since I had scared anyone, but it's like riding a bike—you never forget.

The jingles slowly got louder and louder as I crept through the trees. In the distance I could see a campfire. This was starting to seem more and more like Humans.

As I snuck closer, I realised it wasn't Humans at all! It was a Creeper!

But this wasn't a normal looking Creeper, it was wearing a funny hat and was surrounded by all these **MOOSHROOMS** with sticks coming out of their heads and strange red noses.

Mooshroom madness!

Behind them was a giant sled.
It was sitting off to the side,
decorated with loops and swirls.
It also had a giant sack sitting in
it, and the label on the sack read
'PRESENTS'.

I had never seen anything like it.
What was all this?

'You alright there, Dasher? **HO
HO HO,**' the Creeper asked one
of the funny looking Mooshrooms.

Ho Ho Ho?

It was then that it started to
click for me.

Oh man.

Oh man.

OH MAN!

I knew exactly who this was.

This was **SANTA CREEPS!**

ONE AND A HALF NIGHTS BEFORE CHRISTMAS

Santa!

Real life Santa Creeps!

I guess that Villager that told Steve about Santa being a Creeper in Minecraft was right!

And Santa Creeps had my **PRESENTS!** I counted the days and realised how close Christmas was.

I could just ask for my presents

early! Nothing better than getting your presents before everyone else. Or at least knowing what they were.

Wait until the gang found out that not only had I seen Santa Creeps, but I'd met him and found out what my presents were before everyone else... they would go crazy! I'd be the **COOLEST MOB** in school.

But first I needed some proof. He may have ticked all the boxes, but I needed to make sure that he really was Santa Creeps.

I came out of the shadows.

'Ahem,' I cleared my throat to get the jolly Creeper's attention.

Santa turned around and saw me standing there.

'Hello,' I waved at him.

'Why, hello there!' he said, his voice even jollier than the rest of him. 'Who might you be?'

'My name is Zombie. Zack.' My eyes darted around looking for Santa's **NAUGHTY OR NICE LIST.** 'I've been very good. You don't need to check. I haven't set anything on fire or been kicked out of school or been grounded at all this year. So don't worry about that.'

Santa chuckled. 'I'm sure you've been very good. I guess from that speech, that you know who I am?'

'Yeah, I think I do!' I said, almost **SHAKING** with excitement. 'But I'm gonna need some proof. I can't just believe that every mob with a fancy hat, some funny-looking Mooshrooms and a cool looking sled in the Forest is Santa, you know?'

Real deal?

'Oh, of course!' Santa said. He stood up slowly, then looked around his little campsite, as if he was checking for something. Then he took off his Santa hat and waved it at a log sitting nearby.

SPARKLES floated down from the hat onto the log. Then, the log started flying! It gently whooshed side to side as it rose up in the air, higher and higher. Soon, it was up in the trees, and then above them.

Santa gave the Mooshroom called Dasher a little pat on his side and said, 'Go on, Dasher. Fetch that log.'

Dasher sprung up and started running. It almost looked normal, until Dasher took a step into the air! He was **FLYING!** With each step after that, Dasher climbed higher and higher into the sky. The Mooshroom reached the log, grabbed it with his teeth, turned around and started running down to the ground again.

Wha...?!

By the time Dasher touched down,
my jaw had completely fallen off.

The flying log and Mooshroom... it
had to be **MAGIC!**

'You're kidding me!' I said in shock
as I picked up my jaw off the
ground. 'You really are Santa! Are
you Santa Claus or Santa Creeps?'

Santa chuckled. 'Ahh, the age
old question! We're actually two
different Santas! Santa Claus

gives out presents to Humans, and I give out presents to mobs.'

'Two different Santas?' I asked.

'Of course!' Santa chuckled. 'We can't have mobs like yourself trying to **SCARE** Santa Claus! So it's me who delivers your presents. Just call me Santa Creeps. To what do I owe the pleasure?'

'What? What pleasure? Owing? I don't owe any mob anything, but since you're here, I was wondering if I could get my presents early,' I asked.

'Oh Ho Ho. That'll be a no.' Santa shook his head. 'No presents early—those are the rules.

Only the mobs in the Nether get their presents early because they celebrate on Christmas Eve, but not this early.'

'What's **CHRISTMAS EVE?**'

'That's the night before Christmas,' Santa explained.

'So tonight is Christmas Eve's Eve?'

'Uh... I guess,' Santa shrugged.

'Well I celebrate on Christmas Eve's Eve. So I should get my present now,' I said.

Santa chuckled. 'I may not be from around here, but I wasn't **SPAWNED** yesterday. Plus, at this rate no one will have any presents.'

'Wait, what?!' I shouted.

'I've run into some logistical problems,' Santa sighed.

'I don't know what a logistical is.'

'Basically, the presents aren't

going to get delivered on time. The *Naughty and Nice List* got lost on the way here.' Santa dropped his head to his chest.

'Is it really that important?' I asked.

'I always check over the list before Christmas Eve and now it's far too late for the elves to send another one. How will I deliver all the presents to everyone in Minecraft if we don't know **WHO'S BEEN GOOD AND BAD?'**

'Oh... right. So you have a list of

mob names but no way to put them in the *Naughty or Nice List* without the elves' help?'

'Yes. I don't know how Christmas can go ahead without that list.' Santa shook his head sadly.

A million thoughts raced through my head. Well, maybe not a **MILLION.** Maybe more like three.

Santa didn't know who was good and who was bad! That meant I might still get a present. All I had to do was make sure that

Santa never got that list from the elves... And that Christmas would still go ahead!

'I can help you!' I offered. 'You don't need to get the list from the elves. I know everyone, and I can tell you if they've been good or bad.'

'Hmm,' Santa scratched his chin. **'HOOLEY DOOLEY,** that might just work!' He turned to his Mooshrooms. 'Did you hear that, Dasher? Prancer? Comet? We might still have a chance to pull Christmas off!'

'Woohoo! Let's do it!' I cheered.

'Alright, meet me here tomorrow, okay, Zombie?' Santa Creeps said. 'Tomorrow will be Christmas Eve, so we'll have to be fast if we're going to pull this off.'

I nodded. 'You got it, Santa.'

'And remember—don't tell anyone you've seen me. We'll lose the **MAGIC OF CHRISTMAS** otherwise.'

ONE NIGHT BEFORE CHRISTMAS
(AKA CHRISTMAS EVE)

'Bye, Mum!' I shouted.

'Wait! Zombie! Where are you going?' Mum called out.

'Oh... uh... just to hang out with... Skelee,' I said in a super convincing and confident voice.

Mum nodded. She believed me!

'Okay... well take Wesley with you.'

'Wait, **WHAT?**' I shouted.

'Wesley is old enough to hang out with you and your friends while you play video games,' Mum said. 'I guess that is what you're doing, right?'

'Yeah... but we're gonna play... a **PVP TOURNAMENT.**' I was making this up on the fly.

'Hmm,' Mum shook her head. 'If it's fine for you, it should be fine for Wesley. Take him along, Zombie!'

Mum grabbed Wesley's hand and placed it in mine.

Wesley shook my hand off, then

jumped on his Chicken, Chuck.

'**ABSOLUTELY NOT.** No.
Not happening,' I said, glaring at
them both.

NOOOOOO!

'Fine,' Mum said sighing.

YES! I got out of having to babysit
Wesley.

Mum took Wesley off Chuck's back. 'Chuck stays home. It's just the boys!'

Wesley gave Chuck a little goodbye pat before turning to look at me. 'Let's go, Zumbie!'

UGH!

Once we were out of sight of the house, I pulled Wesley aside. 'Okay, Wesley, you need to go home.'

'But I don't want to, Zumbie,' he said.

'I don't care. You gotta. Just turn around and sneak back into the house.'

'Hmmm... no.'

Wait, what? Wesley is a **CHICKEN JOCKEY,** he's not meant to say no. He's meant to do whatever I say! What was going on?!

'What do you mean "no"?' I asked, gobsmacked. 'I'm older, so you need to do what I say.'

'Well, Mum's older than you. So I should do what she says.' Wesley

grinned a toothy grin at me. 'I
wanna hang out with you.'

I groaned.

I had to meet Santa soon. If Wesley
wasn't gonna leave me alone... well,
I'd have to try and **DITCH HIM.**

'Okay, follow me!' I told Wesley
enthusiastically.

I turned and started walking
towards the Forest.

'What are we going that way for?
Skelee doesn't live in the Forest,'
Wesley said.

I had no idea that Wesley
knew where Skelee lived, but
he was right. Skelee lived in a
MANSION. Definitely not in
the Forest.

'How are you gonna do PVP practice
in the Forest?' Wesley asked.

'Shh. Stop asking questions.'

It wasn't long before Wesley and
I were deep in the Forest. Santa
would be nearby. It was time to
make my move.

'Hey, Wesley! Look at that!' I

pointed at a tree far away in fake amazement.

'What?' Wesley said, spinning to look at the tree.

As soon as he did, I turned and bolted in the opposite direction. I ran and hid behind a tree, then peeked out to check that Wesley turned back and went home.

HANG ON... what?!

Wesley was gone!

I spun in a circle.

Where was Wesley?!

Oh no. No. NO! Mum was gonna kill me if I lost Wesley.

'Hiya, Zumbie.'

'**AAAHHHHH!**' I screamed. 'What did you do that for?'

'Do what?' Wesley grinned.

'Sneak up on me!'

'Aren't we playing hide-and-seek? Anyway, gotcha!' Wesley cackled.

'Haha... yeah, hide-and-seek...'

Okay, that clearly didn't work. If Wesley didn't want to go home, and I couldn't lose him in the Forest, I was just going to have to bring him with me to meet Santa.

'Anyway, we have to keep going,' I said.

'Does Skelee live in the Forest now?' Wesley asked.

'No... Wesley, I'm gonna tell you a **SECRET,** but you can't tell anyone. Especially Mum. You promise not to tell?'

Wesley thought about it for a minute.

'How about Chuck?'

'No, not even Chuck!'

Wesley frowned, but said, 'Okay.'

'Okay... Wesley, we're not going to Skelee's house. We're going to meet... Santa.'

'Who is Santa?'

'A nice old mob who's gonna give everyone in the OVERWORLD a present.'

'Even me?' Wesley asked.

'Even you,' I nodded. 'He needs help getting mobs' presents to them, so we're gonna help him out. But you can't tell anyone.'

Wesley nodded seriously at me. 'I promise I won't tell anyone.'

'Good,' I said. I led him towards the last place I'd seen Santa and his **MOOSHROOM SLEIGH.**

It didn't take long to find him. Santa was in the exact same spot as before, curled up asleep.

'Ahem,' I cleared my throat to get his attention. He didn't wake up. 'Ahem,' I said, a little louder. 'AHEM!!!!'

'Whaaa?!!' Santa sat upright in the sleigh. 'Oh... you! You came back! And you brought a little friend. Hello, I'm Santa Creeps. I hope you're on the Nice List.'

'What's a nice—'

'He's definitely on the Nice List. Are you ready to go?' I said quickly.

CHRISTMAS EVE

'So, where are we going first?' I asked, jumping into the Mooshroom sleigh to sit beside Santa.

'First things first. If you two are helping me deliver presents, you need hats,' Santa explained.

'HATS?' Wesley asked.

He was still trying to climb into the Mooshroom sleigh. Santa picked Wesley up and plonked him into the seat next to me. Then he turned and started digging through the back of the sleigh. After a minute, he stood upright again and used a foot to hold out two bunched up bits of fabric to me and Wesley.

I took the fabric from Santa's foot and unfolded it. I was expecting a hat like Santa's, but this one was red and green instead. I looked at Santa.

'It's an elf hat,' Santa said. 'For Santa's helpers.'

AN ELF HAT!

I tugged mine on and looked at myself in the Mooshroom sleigh's rearview mirror. A couple of **SILVER SPARKLES** had sprinkled onto my arms, and I thought back to when Santa had made the log fly. I looked FABULOUS! AND MAGICAL!

Am I magic now?

Wesley's hat was a bit big for him. It kept slipping down around his earholes. He eventually angled it so that he could peep out from under the red trim.

'Perfect! Now that we're feeling the **CHRISTMAS MAGIC,** we're finally ready to start delivering some presents!' Santa said.

'WOOHOO!' Wesley and I cheered.

'Us first!' I said.

I dove into the back of the Mooshroom sleigh and started

looking through the giant sack labelled 'PRESENTS'.

I saw a giant box with a huge bow. I greedily grabbed it and hoisted it into the air.

'I WANT THIS ONE!' I shouted.

Wesley dived head-first into the present sack and started to go through it too. But before he could find anything, Santa pulled him out of the sack. Santa then **SNATCHED** the giant box out of my hands and gently pushed it back into the sack.

'No, no, no, mobs! That's not how Christmas works. It's about the joy of giving. You get your presents last! After all, truly nice mobs don't care about presents. It's the thought that counts, you know,' Santa said. 'Unless you're not nice Zombies, and you're actually **NAUGHTY ZOMBIES?'**

GULP!

I really wanted first pick of the presents, but it didn't look like that would be happening. And if Santa thought I'd been naughty, then I wouldn't get any presents at all!

'No, no!' I said in a rush, shaking my head. 'We're nice! Super nice.'

Wesley sniffed and his bottom lip started to shake. 'But I want a **PRESEEEEENT!**' he wailed.

Oh no! I started to panic. If Wesley lost the plot, Santa might realise that we're not actually on the Nice List. I had to get Wesley to calm down and go along with whatever Santa said.

'Well, Wesley, if you're so obsessed with presents, you'll never get one, so you might as well go home.' Two birds, one block, I thought. 'I'm not obsessed with presents, that's why I get to stay.'

'So I'll get a present later?' Wesley sniffed. He wiped his **SNOTTY NOSE** on the back of his hand.

'Yeah. But maybe you should go home anyway,' I said, gently pushing him so he slid to the edge of the Mooshroom sleigh.

Wesley gripped tight to the edge of the sleigh and shook his head. 'Nope! I'm coming.'

I groaned. 'Fine! But no more crying.'

Wesley sniffed and sat up straight.

'Well, that's good! We can get started delivering the presents,' Santa said, and handed me a **LONG LIST OF NAMES.**

Dude! That's a long list!

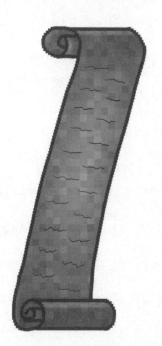

'The first person on the list is...
Principal Hogskins! I know where
she lives.' I couldn't forget that!
I'd staked out her house so I could
get back my confiscated controller.

'And is Principal Hogskins on the
naughty or nice list?' Santa asked.

And that's when it hit me. The
real **POWER** I held in my Zombie
hands.

I don't do very well at school
cause of my pea-sized brain, and
Principal Hogskins is kinda scary
sometimes. But lately she hadn't

been so bad. She *is* gaming royalty, **BO1NKERS,** and she *did* give me insanely good PVP tactics to use. So I suppose she's not so bad that she doesn't deserve a present.

'Nice!' I declared.

'Excellent,' Santa said.

And with that, Santa flicked the reins, and his Mooshrooms tossed their heads. Then, together, they started running. The next thing I knew, the Mooshrooms, the sleigh— all of us—were flying!

This was gonna be the best night ever!

LATER ON CHRISTMAS EVE

Principal Hogskins' house was a breeze. Santa landed the Mooshroom sleigh on the roof of her house with the skill of someone who has spent years driving a Mooshroom sleigh.

As soon as the Mooshrooms' hooves touched down on the roof, Principal Hogskins' **GUARD PIG** started going crazy in her backyard. I hoped it wouldn't wake her up!

Next, Santa pulled the sack of presents out of the back of the sleigh and rummaged through it for a minute.

'This,' Santa said triumphantly, as he pulled a rectangular box out of the sack, 'is Principal Hogskins' **PERFECT** gift.'

The present had a little gift tag hanging off it, with a name scrawled on it. PRINCIPAL HOGSKINS.

Then Santa handed the present to me. 'You should deliver it, Zombie.

The best part of being Santa is leaving the presents!'

'Sure!' I said.

It would probably be some amazing new **GAMING CONSOLE!** Maybe I could hide the present away somewhere and keep it for myself? But I paused my thoughts—Santa would notice and then he would definitely know I wasn't on the Nice List.

Watch out Overworld, there's a new champion in town!

'What do I do?' I asked Santa.

'Slide down the chimney and leave the present under the tree,' he explained. 'There's just one rule— **NO MOB CAN EVER SEE YOU!** It's gotta be a secret, okay?'

'Okay,' I nodded and walked over to the top of the chimney. I looked over the edge at the guard Pig. 'Not this time, little guy.' And with the present in hand, I jumped feet first into the chimney.

I landed gently, with a soft thud.

Which I wasn't expecting. Maybe it was Christmas magic?

I peeked out of the fireplace. The house was exactly as I remembered, but there were loads more **PVP TROPHIES!**

I put the present under her tree and turned back to head up the chimney when I noticed something. It was a plate of cookies and a glass of milk!

I stepped closer and saw a little note next to the snacks.

Dear Santa,

Thanks for the present and for visiting my biome. I hope you come every year now. Please enjoy this glass of milk and these delicious cookies I baked.

Have Yourself a Mouldy Minecraft Christmas!

Principal Hogskins

Hmmf!! *The cookies are for Santa, I thought glumly.*

But wait.

I'M SANTA! Well, for now anyway. I rode in the Mooshroom sleigh and I delivered the presents. That was all the proof I needed.

Without waiting another second,
I shoved as many cookies into my
mouth as I could, then I washed them
all down with the big glass of milk.

That was so yum! Principal
Hogskins definitely deserved to be
on the Nice List.

Once I was back on the roof, I told
Santa and Wesley that the delivery
had gone off without a hitch. I
didn't tell them **ANYTHING**
about the milk and cookies though.

Santa looked at the next name on
the list.

'Next stop, Ellie's house.'

Great! I knew exactly how to get there. She was Creepy's favourite cousin, after all.

Ellie was a **GAMER GENIUS!** She definitely belonged on the Nice List cause of all the times she helped me out so I could win PVP Tournaments.

I told Santa this and he nodded. 'The elves must have thought so too! She has a few presents in the sack. Why don't you take the whole sack down?'

'Sure,' I agreed.

When I got to the bottom of the chimney, I dragged the sack out after me. After searching through it for a while, I found a few presents with Ellie's name on them.

Man, she must have been good to get THREE presents!

But that was when I got distracted by yet another plate of milk and cookies.

This was the best!

I was scoffing them down when I heard a thudding on the staircase.

Oh no! I couldn't let anyone catch me. Especially not Ellie! She was a Creeper and I didn't want to set off another **EXTINCTION LEVEL EVENT.** Not on Christmas Eve. Time to get out of there!

I quickly threw Ellie's presents under the tree, and stuffed the leftover cookies in my pocket.

Just as I got to the fireplace, I

saw some feet appear at the top
of the staircase.

Can't get busted!

I dragged the sack in after me and
the Christmas magic whooshed me
up the chimney to the roof before
Ellie could take a step down.

PHEW.

I stumbled out of the chimney as
the adrenalin ran through me.

'Zombie, are you alright?' Santa asked.

'Ellie almost caught me,' I told him. 'I didn't even have time to finish my cookies!'

'Cookies?!' Wesley yelled. **'I WANT COOKIES!'**

Oh right, Wesley. I forgot about him.

His lower lip started to wobble dangerously. Oh man, he was gonna start crying again.

'Look, Wesley, here.' I pulled a slightly smushed cookie out of my pocket. 'Have this cookie.'

Immediately the wobbly lip and tear-filled eye sockets went away.

Faker.

Wesley grabbed the cookie out of my hand and started munching happily.

At this point, I wouldn't be mad at all if Santa decided that Wesley didn't deserve presents and belonged on the Naughty List.

'More?' Wesley held out a
BOOGER-COVERED HAND.

'I don't have any more.' I emptied my pockets to prove it to Wesley. 'Look, if the next house has cookies, I promise to bring some back for you, okay?'

Wesley frowned, but then nodded and said, 'Okay.'

It was when we were flying to the next house that I realised I would have to share all of my cookies with Wesley now!

Suddenly, I recognised **OUR HOUSE** below us! We were flying pretty low to the ground, so

I took my chance and gave him a quick bump with my hip.

'Oh, careful there, little fella! Don't want to fall out, do we now?' Santa picked Wesley up and popped him between us. Very far from the edge of the Mooshroom sleigh.

SIGH.

EVEN LATER THAT EVE

We finished a few other houses, then stopped at Old Man Jenkins' house. We had to include presents for him, his wife, and their  **ZOMBIE HORSES,** Ed and Dumpling.

Their house was definitely the hardest. As I landed in the fireplace, I realised that Ed and Dumpling were fast asleep in the living room. It looked like they had camped out to see if they could catch Santa, or in this case, me!

Nice horseys

I had to tiptoe around the living room, which, as a Zombie, is really hard to do. Something could **FALL OFF!**

I managed to gently step around the two large Zombie Horses, and leave presents under the tree.

Then, I walked into the fireplace and the magic took me up to the roof with a whoosh!

When I climbed out of Old Man Jenkins' chimney, Santa **HIGH-FIVED** me. We were making great time and he reckoned that I was smashing it. I even brought some cookies back for Wesley so that he stayed quiet and didn't whinge.

Well, that was the goal.

But Wesley was Wesley, and he whinged. He wanted more and more cookies, but my pockets couldn't

fit any more! Brothers are so
annoying.

I was still trying to work out how
ditch him, but Santa was always
watching.

'Onto the next house!' Santa said
in a **JOLLY VOICE.**

Next up on the list was Steve.

'Steve is the best!' I explained
to Santa as I climbed into the
Mooshroom sleigh after him.

'Oh?' Santa said.

Wesley was quietly munching on the four cookies I'd brought back for him.

'Yeah! He helps me all the time and he always has the answers to everything. He's super patient when I don't get things. Did I mention that I have a **PEA-SIZED BRAIN?**'

'Yeah, a few times,' Santa said. He flicked the reins and the Mooshroooms shot up into the air.

'Anyway, he's always been super nice to me and we have really

FUN ADVENTURES. Actually, he's super nice to everyone. I've never seen Steve be mean ever.'
Wow, Steve is actually so nice, he belongs on the Nice List for real...

When we landed on Steve's roof, I jumped down and grabbed the sack of presents.

'Remember now,' Santa said slowly. 'Just because he's your friend, doesn't mean you get to give him all the presents. Just the ones with his name.'

I nodded and picked up the sack

of presents to take down the chimney.

Man! Steve must definitely have been on the Nice List, because the sack was **SUPER HEAVY.** I was carefully placing Steve's presents under his tree, when I heard a THUNK!

I quickly turned around to look at the staircase, but there was no sign of anyone.

PHEW! Steve wasn't coming down the stairs.

I went to grab some cookies for Wesley, but there weren't any.

Huh?

Surely Steve would have left out some cookies!

But there were none on the plate, so I climbed back into the fireplace, and just as the **CHRISTMAS MAGIC** was starting to pull me up the chimney, the sack got caught on something.

What the...?

With a yank, I pulled it free and

was suddenly **WHOOSHED** up to Steve's roof.

I gave Santa a thumbs up that the present drop-off had gone perfectly. 'All done!'

'Perfect!' Santa said. 'Onto the next house!'

After that we went back to Mob Village, and did drop-offs at Creepy, Slimey and Skelee's houses.

I am such a good friend and I told Santa that my friends all deserved presents and were totally good mob kids. Santa would never know that they'd all had detention and been grounded.

It was only when I climbed of the chimney of Skelee's house with a **POCKETFUL OF COOKIES** that I noticed something was wrong.

'Wesley, I have some cookies for you!' I announced.

But he didn't reply.

'Wesley?' I called out.

'Ugh-guff!' Santa had been napping on the sleigh, and woke with a start.

'Santa! Where's Wesley?' I asked.
I started looking all over the sleigh.
I checked behind the seats, under
the sleigh, even in the present sack.

'Wesley?' Santa yawned and
rubbed his eyes.

'My little brother! About this high?'
I said, holding my hand up to show
how tall Wesley was. Anything to
jog Santa's memory.

'Ahh, the COOKIE MUNCHER.'

'YES! Santa, help me look!'

After a few minutes of searching

around the Mooshroom sleigh and
roof, Santa sighed. 'He's not here.'

'What do you mean he's not here?!
He has to be!' I shouted.

What was going on? Where was
Wesley?! I was gonna be in so
much trouble if I lost him. My
parents would **NEVER** forgive me!

Where could he be?

I'm gonna be on
the Naughty List
for life!!!

TWO HOURS TILL CHRISTMAS

'We have to go back!' I told Santa. 'We need to find Wesley.'

'Go back?' Santa shook his head. 'We can't do that. Christmas Eve is almost over and we have to deliver all the presents or mobs won't get their presents in time for Christmas.'

'But I can't leave Wesley. He may be **ANNOYING,** and I hate bringing him along to things, but he's my brother!'

Santa just put his hand on my shoulder. 'I understand. You go find your brother. I can go on without you. There's only a couple of houses left.'

'Thanks, Santa,' I said.

'Do you want me to drop you anywhere?' Santa asked.

'Let me think first.' I paused for a second. Oh no! I'm gonna have to use my BRAIN.

I gotta pretend I'm Wesley. Get into his mind. Where would I go if **I WAS WESLEY?** What would

I think, what would I want?

I braced myself and began to think like Wesley:

HI, MY NAME IS WESLEY.

I LIKE RIDING CHICKENS AND BEING ANNOYING.

I GO PLACES ZUMBIE DOESN'T WANT ME TO GO.

I DO THINGS ZUMBIE DOESN'T WANT ME TO DO.

I WHINGE ALL THE TIME.

I WANT STUFF LIKE ZUMBIE'S VIDEO GAMES AND HIS COOKIES.

I ANNOY HIM ABOUT COOKIES A LOT.

WAIT, THAT'S IT!

Wesley had been annoying me about cookies! He wanted more cookies than what the mobs were leaving out for Santa. He must have snuck off to look for cookies!

But where? Did he know where the cookies were coming from?

Did he realise they were **INSIDE MOB'S HOUSES?!**

'Zombie?' Santa repeated himself. 'Do you want me to drop you somewhere?'

'WAIT HERE, SANTA!' I shouted, then I jumped down the chimney again.

I landed in Skelee's fireplace again. His mansion was SO big. I didn't know how I was going to find Wesley if he'd wandered but my first stop was the cookie table.

'Wesley?' I whisper-shouted. I couldn't raise my voice otherwise Skelee or his housekeepers might wake up, and I'd break Santa's number one rule about not being seen. 'Wesley, I have cookies! Cookies! Come and get them!'

I heard a loud **THUD** upstairs.

Oh no! Someone was waking up!

'Cookies!' I whispered frantically. 'Cookies!!!'

I looked around the tree, under the couch, in the cupboard, but I couldn't find Wesley.

'COOKIES!' I whisper-shouted again.

Suddenly, **HEAVY FOOTSTEPS** were moving around upstairs.

OH NO!

I gave the living room, library and conservatory another scan before deciding that Wesley wasn't there. He would have come out while I was yelling 'cookies' if he was.

I paused for a second before I realised the footsteps upstairs were moving towards the staircase.

Someone was gonna come down the stairs!

Skelee must have been coming to investigate. Just as some **BONY FEET** started to thump their way down the stairs, I jumped into the fireplace and whooshed up to the roof.

Still can't get busted!

Santa looked at me, hope shining in his eyes.

Oh man! He thinks I found Wesley

I didn't say anything, just shook my head sadly.

WESLEY WASN'T THERE.

ONE HOUR TILL CHRISTMAS

After Skelee's house, I asked
Santa to drop me off at Creepy's,
our last stop, before he went off
by himself to finish.

With a lift of his little red hat,
Santa wished me luck. 'I hope you
find your little brother. If you
need me, look up to the moon and
call out **"HO HO HO"**. But
only tonight. Not always, you know?
I'm busy other nights of the year.'

'Thanks, Santa,' I said.

'C'mon Prancer, Blitzen, Dancer and everyone else!' Santa flicked the reins of the Mooshroom sleigh, but then pulled back on them to stop the sleigh. 'I almost forgot.' Santa pointed at his head and then held out his foot.

Oh man! I forgot about **SANTA'S MAGIC ELF HAT.**

'Onwards!' The Mooshrooms tossed their heads and started to run. Just as the Mooshroom sleigh reached the edge of the roof, it slipped up into the night sky led by the Mooshrooms.

I watched for a moment as Santa and the Mooshroom sleigh got further and further away, disappearing into the biome to deliver the last few presents.

I was alone and I needed to find Wesley! The poor little guy was **LOST** and probably nervous.

I started searching around the roof, but to be honest there wasn't much to search for. The roof was empty except for some tiles and the top of the chimney.

I decided that I needed to look

inside Creepy's house in case Wesley had snuck in there.

I jumped into the chimney and—

'AAAGGHHHHHHHH!!'

BANG!!

What the...?!

That had been a lot different from my last trip down a chimney.

I'd forgotten that without the Christmas hat I wouldn't be able to float gently down the chimney and land softly.

I quickly pulled myself together.

Get over here legs!

Suddenly I saw **LIGHTS** turn on upstairs.

Oh no! I must have shouted too loudly when I fell down the chimney!

'Cookies! Cookies! Wesley? Cookies!' I

whisper-shouted.

I quickly spun through the room, but I couldn't find Wesley. I ran back to the chimney and climbed into the fireplace.

I jumped, expecting to shoot out of the chimney but landed on... the ground? The jump did **NOTHING!**

I saw more lights go on upstairs. I needed to get out of the house!

I did another small jump. And another. And another.

But I was **TRAPPED** without Santa's magic hat.

There was no other choice. I made a mad dash for the front door, pulled it open and ran through before slamming it behind me. That was too close!

But I could still hear the sound of footsteps running down the stairs to the door behind me. I took off running so fast that I ran straight into a washing line where clothes were hanging out to dry!

'AAAGHH!' I screamed, as black

suddenly surrounded me. I wiggled and thrashed and kept running. As I ran, I finally untangled myself from the washing to realise I was wrapped in **CREEPY'S DAD'S PANTS...** again!

NOT AGAIN!!!

I tied them around my waist but kept running till I was far enough away, then I dived and hid behind a bush.

I turned around to see the lights on all through Creepy's house. **PHEW!** Lucky he didn't catch me!

Once the thrill of having escaped Creepy's house disappeared, I remembered I hadn't found Wesley.

Where could he be?!

30 MINUTES TILL CHRISTMAS

I walked from Creepy's house back to Slimey's house. I followed the exact path of the sky-route me and Santa and the Mooshroom sleigh had taken. As I walked, I called out to Wesley.

'Cookies! I have COOKIES!' I kept my **EYE SOCKETS** peeled in case my brother was around. 'Wesley?!'

I got to Slimey's house and still hadn't found Wesley.

I was starting to lose hope. It would be Christmas soon!

As I circled Slimey's house, I realised that they had left a window open.

I thought of Creepy's dad's pants wrapped around me and the open window and had **AN IDEA!**

I pulled Creepy's dad's pants back over my head to use it as a mask. That way no one would know it was me even if they did see me.

With my **PANTS-MASK** on, I crawled and pulled my way through the window of the house.

I whispered and looked for Wesley. I didn't bump into anything or scream or attract any attention, and no one came downstairs.

But I still didn't find Wesley.

As I gently pulled myself out of the same window, I saw soft rays of light coming across the sky.

Oh no. It was almost daylight!

I was so torn. Did I keep looking for Wesley or did I go home to hide from the sunlight in safety?

I didn't know what to do.

While I sat and tried to think, the sun rose higher and higher in the sky.

It took me so long to think that I didn't have a choice anymore. I had to run home or I'd **BURST INTO FLAMES!** All I could do was hope that Wesley had found a safe spot to hide from the sun. I ran like my Zombie legs had never run before!

CHRISTMAS NIGHT

'Zombie! Wake up! It's time for presents!' my mum gently called from the doorway.

I groaned. I hadn't slept a wink all day for worrying about Wesley.

My parents had trusted me with him and I had **LOST** him!

I hadn't even checked under the tree when I got home. And I didn't even want to open presents now.

My little brother could be **ZOMBIE ASHES** somewhere.

'Zombie!' Mum shook my shoulders. 'Wake up! Let's go open the Christmas presents.'

'Mum,' I said, sitting up. 'I don't want to open presents. I have to tell you something.'

'What? You don't want to open presents? But you love presents! I thought you were so excited. I heard you talking about Christmas to your friends, so I thought you would want to wake your brother to open presents first thing!'

'I don't want to open presents because... because... because I lost Wesley! **WAAAAHHHHH!! WAAAAAAHH!! WAAAAHH!**' I started bawling. 'You trusted me and I lost him!'

'You lost Wesley?' Mum said, shocked. 'He isn't in his room?'

'No,' I sniffed. 'He came on an adventure with me and I lost him. But I promise, now that it's dark again, I'm gonna go back out and keep looking for him!'

'What do you mean, "an adventure"?' Mum asked.

I paused. I didn't know if I should tell her, cause Santa had told me not to tell anyone.

But that was before Wesley got lost. And Wesley was more important than some **SECRET.**

I sniffed again. 'We were with Santa Creeps,' I said quietly.

'Santa Creeps?' Mum repeated. 'You mean the mob who brought us all those presents?'

'Yeah.' I nodded, wiping my booger.

I was about to throw away the tissue, but I realised it was a pretty **GOOD-LOOKING BOOGER.** I decided to keep it for my booger collection.

'I met Santa Creeps and he told me the *Naughty and Nice List* was lost in the post. So I thought that if I helped him, then I wouldn't end up on the Naughty List and I'd still get a present. But then you made me take Wesley and I lost him!'

'Oh, Zombie!' Mum said. 'Everyone deserves presents on Christmas!'

'Really?' I asked her. 'So I won't get a lump of Coal or be grounded?'

Then Mum got **FLAMES** in her eyes and I knew I was in trouble.

UH OH!

'I don't know about this lump of Coal, but you're definitely grounded.

Just as soon as we find Wesley.'

'I can look for him,' I offered.

Mum immediately stood up. 'We're ALL going to look for him!'

'I'm sorry,' I sniffled. 'I didn't mean to lose him.'

'I know,' Mum said. 'And Wesley is a **RESOURCEFUL MOB,** I'm sure he'll be alright.'

'What does resourceful mean?' I sniffed. 'Does it mean he's gonna roast?'

'Nope!' Mum shook her head.
'Resourceful means that he'll have
found a way to stay safe from the
sun. He will be okay. We just have
to find him!'

Mum, Dad and I split up to search
for Wesley. They went to look
around the Forest, while I looked
around **MOB VILLAGE.**

I felt bad breaking my promise
to Santa, but Wesley was more
important to me than his secret.
In fact, I didn't realise how

important Wesley was to me. It was almost as if I... I... I might love him? He's my brother and he's **SUPER ANNOYING,** but yeah, I guess I do love him!

'Zombie!' a voice called out.

I turned and saw Creepy, Skelee and Slimey coming towards me. They waved excitedly.

I waved weakly.

'What's going on?' Skelee asked as they got closer. 'Were your presents bad?'

'Ours were weird,' Slimey said.

'Yeah, that **SANTA DUDE** got ours mixed up!' Creepy laughed.

'What?' I didn't think I had gotten any mobs' presents mixed up. 'What're you guys talking about?'

'Santa!' Creepy said. 'One of Slimey's presents got left at mine.'

Oh, whoops.

'And guess what?' Skelee said. 'I think I heard Santa at my place!'

Ahh, double whoops.

'Whaddya mean?' I asked, as coolly as I could.

'I heard him! He made a massive noise and was yelling about cookies!' Skelee explained.

'Oh, NO WAY!' Creepy shouted.

'YES WAY!' Skelee laughed.

'Dude, you won't believe it—the exact same thing happened to me!' Creepy said.

TRIPLE WHOOPS.

'Really?' Skelee, Slimey and I asked together.

'Crashing noises and **YELLING ABOUT COOKIES!** Santa definitely visited both of us!' Creepy laughed.

Slimey frowned. 'I just got presents. No yelling about cookies. Although he did eat all the cookies that I left out for him.'

'Anyway, why are you sad?' Skelee asked me again.

'Oh,' I said. I had forgotten about missing Wesley for a minute. 'It's not my presents,' I said, answering their earlier question. 'I haven't even opened my presents.'

'You haven't opened them? Not even a squeeze to feel the shape or a shake to hear how it rattles?' Slimey asked.

I shook my head. 'I didn't want to, cause... cause... cause I lost Wesley! **WAAAAH!!**' I started to wail. I just couldn't stop, I was so sad.

'Oh man,' Skelee said. 'Do you want our help to look for him? He's a smart little Chicken Jockey. I'm sure he'll be just fine.'

'Thanks, guys,' I sniffed.

The guys tried to cheer me up as we looked for Wesley. I had to lead them along the route I had taken with Santa last night, without telling them why we were going that way. I may have told Mum and Dad about Santa, but I couldn't tell my FRIENDS!

We had been looking for a little while when we reached the edge of the Forest and I heard the familiar THUNK! THUNK! THUNK! of

Steve chopping down trees.

'I'm gonna go check in with Steve.
I'll catch up with you guys later?'
I suggested.

'Sure,' Slimey, Skelee and Creepy
nodded. 'We'll keep looking for
Wesley till then.'

'THANKS, GUYS!'

It didn't take long to find the
clearing Steve was chopping Wood
in.

'Heya, Steve,' I called out.

'ZOMBIE!' Steve said excitedly.
'MERRY CHRISTMAS!'

'Thanks,' I said sadly.

'Zombie, I have a present for you. A little surprise!' Steve said enthusiastically.

'That's okay, I'm not really in the mood for presents,' I said, shaking my head.

'No, trust me, you'll want this present!' Steve said. 'Here.'

Steve held out a giant lump wrapped in red, topped with a little elf hat.

Hang on, that elf hat looked familiar...

'ZUMBIE!'

'WESLEY?!' I shouted.

Wesley wriggled out of the wrapping paper and Steve's hands and ran towards me excitedly.

BEST. PRESENT. EVER!!!

I knelt down and wrapped him in a hug. 'Wesley! I can't believe you're here!'

'Zumbie!' Wesley yelled happily around a **MOUTHFUL OF COOKIE.**

Wait.

Cookie?

I looked at Steve.

Steve was grinning at me. 'I found little Wesley when I woke up on Christmas. He was munching on the cookies I left for Santa and was pretty chatty.'

I just laughed.

'It was pretty **LUCKY** I found him and not one of the other Villagers. But we had a great time waiting for the sun to set so I could bring him to you, didn't we, buddy?'

Wesley looked back a Steve, grinning through chewed up cookie bits.

'I can't believe it! I knew I'd left him somewhere along the way.'

'Wesley told me everything. I can't believe you met Santa! And hung out with him! How was he?' Steve asked.

'He was a Creeper called Santa Creeps and his sleigh was pulled by Mooshrooms.'

'Amazing,' Steve said. 'That Villager was right!'

I just kept hugging Wesley.

I never thought I would be so happy to see this **LITTLE ZOMBIE.** I would really, really miss him if he was gone!

'Is Christmas always this **EXCITING?**' I asked Steve.

'Nah. Normally you just eat a whole bunch, then open a heap of presents. I've never had to reunite family members.'

'Yeah, I thought this Christmas seemed pretty special,' I said, picking Wesley up.

'Anyway, what presents did you get?' Steve asked. He held a shiny new Axe by his side.

'Oh man! I forgot to leave me and Wesley a present!'

PLOP!

Two somethings dropped from the sky and landed next to my feet.

Finally, presents!

One said WESLEY and smelt suspiciously like cookies. The other present tag said:

To Zombie,

Looks like you found what you were looking for, and so did I.

Thank you for all your help.

Have Yourself a mouldy Minecraft Christmas.

SC

I opened the box and found a rolled-up piece of paper.

'What's that, Zumbie?' asked Wesley.

'I don't know, buddy.' I unrolled the scroll and found... the Naughty and Nice List.

NAUGHTY	NICE
~~ZOMBIE~~	STEVE
~~WESLEY~~	SLIMEY
	CREEPY
	SKELEE
	ELLIE
	PRINCIPAL HOGSKINS
→	ZOMBIE
→	WESLEY